Anonymous

The Right Honourable Annuitant Vindicated With a Word or

Two

in favour of the other great man, in case of his resignation - in a letter to a

friend in the country

Anonymous

The Right Honourable Annuitant Vindicated With a Word or Two
in favour of the other great man, in case of his resignation - in a letter to a friend in the country

ISBN/EAN: 9783337409937

Printed in Europe, USA, Canada, Australia, Japan

Cover: Foto ©Andreas Hilbeck / pixelio.de

More available books at **www.hansebooks.com**

THE

E IGHT HONOURABLE

ANNUITANT

INDICATED.

WITH

A Word or two in Favour of the *other*
GREAT MAN, in Cafe of his
RESIGNATION.

In a LETTER to

FRIEND in the COUNTRY.

LONDON:
Printed for J. MORGAN, in *Pater-nofter Row*.
MDCCLXI.

THE

RIGHT HONOURABLE

ANNUITANT

VINDICATED.

DEAR SIR,

Herewith I fend you the *London Gazette*, by which you will fee that the important paragraphs of news, to which you would not give any credit in the common papers, are confirmed by the higheft authority. I am always forry to differ from you in opinion; but cannot help thinking that on this occafion you

B   have

have exerted lefs than your ufual cando **.
The *Great Commoner* has, in my mind,
thrown up his employments with the
fame honour and the fame fpirit of difin-
tereftednefs that he took them up. He
has retired with only a new dignity an-
nexed to his family, and an ANNUITY,
fo fmall, fo very inconfiderable and inade-
quate to the purpofes of luxury and corruption, that he has been obliged to fet
his Coach Horfes to fale by publick Ad-
vertifement. There is nothing fo moving,
faith *Seneca*, as a great man in diftrefs.
What can be more melancholy than a ftatefman on the *pavèe*?—Yet has our bright
Sun of Patriotifm fet with no lefs glory
than he rofe. He has received the Royal
Thanks—he was *very near* receiving the
City Thanks—and has gone out of power

with

with the fame *unembarraſſed Countenance*
that he came in.

There are, I think, three modes of mi-
niſterial Reſignation. The firſt is, when a
Great Patriot conceives a diſguſt at the baſe-
neſs of any meaſures propoſed by his com-
panions in the Adminiſtration, and from a
noble indignation quits their fellowſhip,
leſt his countrymen ſhould account him
a ſharer in their guilt.—This ſeems to be
the moſt ſimple and natural method, but
is nevertheleſs much the moſt uncom-
mon. The ſecond is, when a Miniſter,
in the ſtile of the news-papers, *reſigns,*
but is, in good truth, fairly *turned out.*—
This method has been practiſed within
all our memories. The third is, when a
Miniſter, for the convenience of the Go-

vernment,

vernment, refigns by private compact and agreement, and receives a certain *douceur* for his compliance.——This, thanks to the complaifance and humanity of the times, is the moft modern mode : and to this the pliant and amiable temper of our GREAT COMMONER has chofen to fubmit.

But this, it feems, it is, which, being barely fuggefted in a news-paper, was capable of alarming you fo fenfibly, and of touching you to the quick with indignation and furprife.——What mere Weathercocks are you Country Gentlemen !——Once you looked upon this fhining Meteor in politicks with diflike. Afterwards; on his efforts to make his way into the cabinet, and take the reins of power into his hands, you feconded his attempts, threw your whole

weight

weight into his fcale, and prompted every corporation in *England* to honour him with their freedom in gold-boxes. But now you revert to your firft principles, and begin to revive your antient fentiments of difapprobation.—And why? or wherefore?—. In order to give your arguments, fuch as they are, fair play, fuffer me to ftate all that you have urged, or can urge, in cenfure of the conduct of our Great Commoner.

Firft then, you may fay, that it is very unlike a Patriot to retire from the Adminiftration of public affairs, at a time when the nation appears to be moft in want of his affiftance.—That to fay he refigned his employments becaufe he found it impoffible to render to his country fuch fervices as he intended, is a weak plea; fince it is

evident

evident, that had he refigned them in a *proper manner*, the voice of the people would have obliged him to refume them, and the meafures he propofed, if at all plaufible, would certainly have been perfued.

Secondly, That to retire with a PENSION, was to retire with ignominy and difgrace, in direct contradiction to the principles, which he has all along fo openly avowed and profeffed.

To give thefe arguments the more force, let us fuppofe, That on the propofal of fuch terms to our GREAT COMMONER, as he appears to have accepted, that he, with the voice and gefture of *Demofthenes*, had replied fomewhat in the following manner.

4   " No.

" No.—Far be it from me ever to affent
' to terms, fo derogatory to my honour,
" fo unworthy of a Lover of his Country!
" Terms, at whofe abject meannefs I am
" fhocked and difgufted, and whofe CRI-
" MINALITY I confider with horrour:—
" Terms, *which would hang, like a* MILL-
" STONE, *about the neck of the Minifter,*
" who fhould difgrace himfelf by his ac-
" ceptance of them, and plunge him into
" the loweft gulph of popular contempt.—
" What part of my conduct could ever
" infpire my moft bitter enemy with the
" lighteft hope that I could be *bought off*
" from my duty, or that my name fhould
" ever be enrolled in the catalogue of PEN-
" SIONERS? Have I not always endea-
" voured to diftinguifh myfelf by my con-
" tempt of money?—Did I not publickly

" re-

" refign to better ufes the perquifites of
" lucrative employments !—And was not
" the firft confiderable acquifition to my
" fortune evidently made by the integrity
" of my conduct, and the fteadinefs of my
" oppofition, to the meafures of corrup-
" tion and venality ?—Whence, I befeech
" you, is the annual Sum, to which this
" PENSION amounts, to iffue ?—It muft
" neceffarily be taken either from the pub-
" lic money or the Civil Lift.--And fhall I
" lie like a burden or heavy impoft on the
" People; or fuffer myfelf or my family
" to become a Rent-Charge on the King?—
" No! it would ill become me, after fuch
" a condefcenfion, to take my feat again in
" *that houfe*, where I have fo often decla-
" red, That it would be better for that
" houfe,

"s houfe *, *if new parliaments were more*
" *frequent, and few Placemen, and No* PEN-
" SIONERS *admitted.*——Or with what grace
" can I permit my Practice to contradict
" my Theory, and prevail on myfelf to
" contribute towards running the Civil Lift
" into debt ? when I have alfo laid it down
" as a maxim, that, ‡ *It is inconfiftent with*
" *the honour of this nation to have our King*
" *ftand indebted to his fervants or tradefmen,*
" *who may be ruined by a delay of payment :*
" *The Parliament has provided fufficiently*
" *for preventing this difhonour's being brought*
" *upon the nation ; and if the Provifion we*
" *have made fhould be* MISAPPLIED *or* LA-
" VISHED, *we muft fupply the deficiency ; we*
" *ought to do it, whether the king makes*

* *Chandler's* Debates, vol. xiii. p. 172.
‡ Ibid. p. 214.

C   *any*

" *any application for that purpose, or no.——*
": After fuch a declaration I fhould blufh to
" divert the ftream of his M—y's munifi-
" cence into fo mean a channel, or to draw
" my life and being from that fource.   I,
" that ftood againft corruption in my youth,
" will not fet my integrity to bargain and
" fale in my old age; for,* *much, very much,*
" *is he to be abhorred, who, as he has ad-*
" *vanced in age, has receded from Virtue,*
" *and becomes more wicked with lefs Tempta-*
" *tion ; who proftitutes himfelf for money*
" *which he cannot enjoy, and fpends the re-*
" *mains of his life in the ruin of his country.*
" Rather, therefore, let me cherifh ‡ *that*
" *Zeal for the fervice of my country, which*
" *neither* HOPE *nor* FEAR *fhall influence me*
" *to fupprefs. I will not fit* UNCONCERNED
" *while my Liberty is invaded, nor look in fi-*
" *lence*

* *Chandler's* Debates, vol. xii. p. 282.
‡ Ibid. p. 283.

" *lence upon* PUBLIC ROBBERY. *I will*
" *exert my endeavours, at whatever hazard,*
" *to repel the Aggreſſor, and drag the Thief*
" *to Juſtice, whoever may protect them in their*
" *villainy, and whoever may partake of their*
" *plunder.*"

In theſe rhetorical flouriſhes I think is contained all that can be advanced, with the leaſt juſtice or propriety, in cenſure of the conduct of our illuſtrious commoner; nor can it be denied but that I have given them their full force, ſince I have introduced many of his own words, and ſome of thoſe notable ſentiments which he himſelf once vollied out, with all the dreadful artillery of eloquence, againſt the GREAT MAN of that day. But then it muſt be remembered, that we have not yet heard him on the

C 2   other

other fide of the queftion. We have not
yet feen him levelling the thunder of his
oratory againft the enemies of placemen
and Penfioners. It is uncandid and ungenerous to condemn him, before you have
heard what he has to fay in his defence.
Audi alteram partem! If, in confirmity to
your fuggeftions, I have forced thefe words
into his mouth again, I warrant you, he is
capable of eating them, ay, and of digeft-
ing them into the bargain. It is not the
firft time, that he has fpoke in favour of
thofe very meafures, which he once reviled; and having firft taught us to hold
them in abomination, afterwards reconci-
led us to his purfuit of them. If, after
the warmeft declarations againft *continental*
connections—if after the ftrongeft oppofition
to remitting either men or money to *Ger-*

many

many, and a downright refusal to consent to give the D--ke of *C———d* any assistance there, though in the most deplorable circumstances—If, I say, after all this, he could himself embrace *continental connections*, if he could send over men by ten thousands, and money by hundred thousands, and nobody be in the least offended or surprized—-why may not he also, who has railed so long at PENSIONS and PENSIONERS, at last take a PENSION *himself*, and prove to the satisfaction of the whole world, that it is not the *thing done*, but the *how*, and the *why*, and the *when*, and by *whom* it is *done*, that constitutes the CRIMINALITY and offence!—May he not tell us, that three thousand pounds *per* Year is a poor reward for all his great and important services? And may he not consider it as a kind

of

of petty tribute from his rich conquests in the *East* and *West Indies*, on the Coast of *France*, and on the *Ocean?* May he not plead his right to an *Otium cum dignitate?* May he not convince us of our mistake in imagining that VIRTUE *is its own reward?* and may he not tell us, that if we suppose the streets of *London* to be paved with silver and gold, we are as much to blame, as he is now sensible he was himself, when he pronounced the streets of *Oxford* to be *paved with Disaffection* and *Jacobitism?*

These things, with many others of equal weight, would undoubtedly suggest themselves to our GREAT MAN, even in an *extempore* reply to the charge brought against him, and even if it was taken on your own representation. But the accufation is not fairly laid. He is neither unjuſt nor inconſiſtent. He has inveighed againſt PENSIONERS, it is true; and he may ſtill continue to do ſo, for he has *no* PEN- SION.—No! what then ?—Why, Sir, he has *an* ANNUITY—An ANNUITY—Not a bit of a PENSION, I aſſure you—for, as *Foigard* wiſely diſtinguiſhes, " if you take " it *beforehand* it is a BRIBE, but if you " take it *afterwards, it is only a* GRATI- " FICATION."—This is no *Bribe,* but a *Reward,* as witneſs *Quebec, Louiſburg, Se- negal, Goree, Guadalupe, Belliſle, &c. &c. &c. &c. &c. &c. &c.*—and is indeed no more than, when an old faithful ſervant gives warning that he will *leave his place,* juſt kindly diſmiſſing him with a month's wages. He has taken an ANNUITY then it is true, but no PENSION—only an AN-

NUITY for his own life; his Lady's life, and the life of his eldest Son—that is, an ANNUITY *for three lives*, for which I heard a Broker at *Jonathan's* say, that he would give Fifty Thousand Pounds, if it ever came into the Alley. An ANNUITY may also have some other properties different from a PENSION. PENSIONS are subject to a Tax—an ANNUITY may perhaps be exempt from this inconvenience, and be established to be paid out of the privy purse *clear of all deductions:* and in that case, if it should ever go to market, my friend at *Jonathan's* must allow that the Purchase-money would be still more considerable.—It must be allowed therefore that a PENSION and an ANNUITY are no more the same thing than an Egg and a Chicken—a *Pension* is but an *Annuity* in

embrio,

embrio, but an *Annuity* is a *Penfion* brought to perfection and maturity.—At the firft exhibition of a *ridotto* in this country, the people were confounded at the novelty of the term, and did not know what it meant : upon which a wag ftuck a paper to the back of one of the company, fignifying, in large letters, *this is the* RIDOTTO. In like manner I would humbly propofe, in order to diftinguifh this GREAT MAN from the mean *Band of Penfioners*, that a label be fixed to his back, with an infcription wrought in gold letters, like the G. R. on the cloaths of the beef-eaters, fignifying in magnificent capitals, THIS IS THE ANNUITANT.

I am forry, my dear fir, that you force me to ftop here to anfwer the contraft

D you

you have drawn between this *Great Man*
and the other gentleman, who was ho-
noured at the same time with himfelf,
with the gold boxes.—He, you fay, retired without any *Penfion*, nay even without
an *Annuity*; and refufed all reward or con-
fideration for his fervices, except a title
for his Lady, to which fhe had a kind of
hereditary claim. Why, Sir—if this be
true—I —I — I — that is——to be fure
——you know, Sir—there is fome kind
of——In fhort I cannot difpute this point
with you. Yet, notwithstanding your
partiality to the gentleman you have in-
ftanced, you muft allow that his political
reputation has always been infinitely infe-
rior to that of our *Great Man*. He has
been no man of *words*, but of *deeds* only.
His patriotifm never made *that noife* in the
world

world which was occasioned by that of his colleague ; and therefore could not fo well afford fuch a drawback from his fame. On the whole, I may venture to allow your friend to be in this inftance the fuperior character, and yet efteem the Great Commoner, *in the main*, as the moft eminent and illuftrious.—As to the dignity, in that affair he has behaved with as much modefty as his friend—nay, with ftill more—for the title by which he has chofen to diftinguifh his lady—*Lady Chat'em*——feems as if taken in jeft——It founds as ridiculous as king of *Brentford*, and feems merely calculated for one of the mock dignitaries in the *Dramatis Perfonæ* of a Comedy.

Prudence is univerfally allowed to be a great virtue—one of the cardinal vir-

tues

tues—and yet, by I know not what fatality, it often encounters contempt, and is received with much lefs admiration than the three other cardinal virtues of *Juftice*, *Temperance*, and *Fortitude*: though after all, Juftice could in real life never make any thing more than a judge ; Temperance is a mere valetudinarian ; and Fortitude a captain in the *militia* at beft ; while Prudence might make a general, a ftatefman, a monarch, or any illuftrious character under the fun. Prudence is the very life and foul of a GREAT MAN; and in the refignation of our illuftrious Commoner, no virtue was more confpicuous than his Prudence. He *prudently* forefaw that there would be much trouble and difficulty in fettling a peace to the liking of all ranks of people; wherefore he very

prudently

prudently quitted his employments; and afterwards very *prudently* also accepted a handsome provision for himself and his family.

Finding my brain big with matter on this part of the vindication of our GREAT MAN's character, and teeming with argument (infomuch that I am only confused by the multiplicity of my materials, and at a lofs in what manner to arrange what I have to fay) juft at this time an ineftimable original, moft curious both as to its ftile and matter, has offered itfelf, which not only corroborates all that has or can be advanced, but ferves alfo to difpofe my fentiments into method and order. The Country Journal of your own County has, I dare fay, copied it from

from our *London* papers, where I found it; but as I shall naturally make many references and allusions to it, it may be more convenient to have it all immediately before you. I have therefore transcribed it in this place.

A Letter from a Right Hon. Person to his Friend in the City.

DEAR SIR,

' FINDING, to my great Surprise, that the Cause and Manner of my ' resigning the Seals, is grosly misrepre-
' sented in the City, as well as that the ' most gracious and *spontaneous* Marks of ' his Majesty's Approbation of my Ser-
' vices, which Marks followed my Re-
' signation, have been infamously traduced

' as

' as a Bargain for my forsaking the Pub-
' lick, I am under a Necessity of declar-
' ing the Truth of both these Facts, in a
' Manner which I am sure no Gentle-
' man will contradict: A Difference of
' Opinion with regard to Measures to be
' taken against *Spain*, of the highest Im-
' portance to the Honour of the Crown,
' and to the most essential national In-
' terests, (and this founded on what *Spain*
' had already done, not on what that
' Court may farther intend to do) was
' the Cause of my resigning the Seals.
' Lord TEMPLE and I submitted, in
' Writing, and signed by us, our most
' humble Sentiments to his Majesty, which
' being over-ruled by the united Opinion
' of all the rest of the King's Servants, I
' resigned the Seals on Monday the 5th of
' this

‘ this Month, in Order not to remain re-
‘ fponfible for Meafures, which I was no
‘ longer allowed to guide. Moft graci-
‘ ous publick Marks of his Majefty’s Ap-
‘ probation of my Services followed my
‘ Refignation: They are unmerited and
‘ unfolicited, and I fhall ever be proud to
‘ have received them from the beft of
‘ Sovereigns.

‘ I will now only add, my dear Sir,
‘ that I have explained thefe Matters only
‘ for the Honour of Truth, not in any
‘ View to court return of Confidence from
‘ any Man, who with a Credulity, as
‘ weak as it is injurious, has thought fit
‘ haftily to withdraw his good Opinion,
‘ from one who has ferved his Country
‘ with Fidelity and Succefs; and who
‘ juftly

'juftly reveres the upright and candid
'Judgment of it; little folicitous about the
'cenfures of the Capricious and the Un-
'generous: Accept my fincereft Acknow-
'ledgments for all your kind Friendfhip,
'and believe me ever with Truth and
'Efteem,

   'My Dear Sir,

     'Your faithful Friend, &c.'

And now, my dear Sir, let me afk you,
if every word of this moft valuable letter does not afford a ftrong confirmation
of our Great Man's Prudence. It affords
alfo an equal proof of his candour and
veracity, *which I am fure no Gentleman
will contradict:* for it *declares the Truth of
both thefe Facts* to be, juft what we all

E   con-

conceived it to be before this epiftle to
his friend in the City was made publick.
Perhaps, however, you rough boifterous
country gentlemen might mifapprehend
this matter. You might poffibly imagine,
that he went bluntly to his Mafter, and
faid, " Sir, if you will give me an *An-*
" *nuity* of three thoufand *per* year, I will
" refign,"—and fo the Bargain was ftruck.
—But how little agreeable would fuch a
conduct be to his *Prudence?* Mark, how
different the cafe really was.. *Moft gra-*
cious publick marks of approbation of my
fervice FOLLOWED *my refignation. Fol-*
*lowed—.*Sir, do you obferve ?—and he
knew that they *would follow* if he chofe
it—To be fure, he did; and there, Sir,
there was the *Prudence.. They* (that is the
Marks) *are unmerited and unfolicited*——

here

here again, Sir, his Prudence and Fore-fight are remarkable—He very *prudently* left *unfolicited* that which he knew would *follow,* and which he knew that he would not refufe. Modeftly, therefore, to fay *they are* UNMERITED, means no more than the *Nolo Epifcopari* of a Bifhop E-lect, who is neverthelefs equally fure of his Epifcopacy.—Your inflexible *Britifh* Spirit, ftubborn as our Oak itfelf, may perhaps feel itfelf offended at fome of the following expreffions. *Lord T. and I fubmitted in Writing, and figned by us, our moft humble fentiments to his Majefty, which being over-ruled by the united Opinion of all the reft of the King's Servants, I refigned the Seals on Monday the 5th of this Month, in order not to remain refponfible*

for

for Measures, which I was no longer al-
lowed to GUIDE.——This, perhaps, you
will fay, is acting and talking like his
Mafter's Mafter, inftead of his humble
Servant, a kind of Lord Paramount over
both K—g and M——y.——Not at all.
—Every fervant of his M——y, as well
as of any other perfon in *England*, is
at liberty to leave his *Place* when he
pleafes; and to leave it juft when there is
the moft need of his affiftance, only tends
to heighten his confequence, and to fhew
that he is *one who has ferved his country*
with FIDELITY *and* SUCCESS.—Did not
feveral of the Greateft Men in the kingdom defert his late M——y, and throw
up their employments, juft when he was
moft in need of their fervices? and were
not they all reinftated in their places?

4   May

May not therefore the GREAT MAN of our times too refign in the very Crifis of our affairs? and though he refufes to do any more for us, need he alfo refufe a reward for what he has done?—Well but then—*Meafures, which I was no longer allowed to* GUIDE.—Thefe, my friend, thefe, I fee, are the words which you cannot digeft, and which you think unbecoming the mouth of a private fubject, nay almoft even of a K—g in this country.——But let not your high ftomach be offended at them. Our GREAT MAN has always habituated himfelf to a Grandeur of expreffion, as well as an elevation of fentiment. It would not be aftonifhing therefore, if he fhould now and then appear fomewhat abfolute; but in the prefent inftance, he is a pattern of

humility.

humility.—Take the whole fentence together, you will find that it is entirely
metaphorical, and will admit of the
mildeft interpretation. *Lord* T. *and I fubmitted in Writing, and figned by us, our moft
humble Sentiments to his Majefty, which being over-ruled by the united opinion* of all
the reft of the King's Servants, *I refigned
the Seals on Monday the 5th of this Month,
in order not to remain refponfible for meafures, which I was no longer allowed to* GUIDE.
Here you fee he confiders the council as fo
many fervants in a family. One perhaps as
the *Maitre d'hotel,* another as the Butler, a
third as my lord's *own man,* and the reft
as fo many footmen, helpers, *&c.* To himfelf he feems to have affigned the province
of the *Coachman;* and, in this fituation,
he has a right to remonftrate againft their

pro-

proceedings: for to propofe *meafures, which
he is no longer allowed to* GUIDE, while he
is yet upon the box, is abfolutely taking the
whip and reins out of his hands. Suppofe you were in your Coach and Six on a
long journey in the middle of winter, in
deep roads and bad weather, and that on
the coachman's preparing to fhew his fkill
in driving to an inch by the edge of a precipice, *the reft of the fervants* were to bawl
out to him to ftop, and you yourfelf fhould
infift on his going another way : In thefe
circumftances, Sir, only fuppofe that the
Coachman was to defcend from his box, and
coming to the coach door accoft you in
thefe terms : " Sir, You have been *the*
" *beft of mafters* to me, it is true, but if I
" go any other way than my own, I'll be
" d——d.—I never overturned you in my
" life,

" life, and if you will *no longer allow me*
" *to* GUIDE, why then, by G—d, neither
" I, nor the *Poſtillion,* will drive you an
" inch further, and ſo you may get home
" as you can."—Now, Sir, in ſuch a caſe,
though you might not chuſe to run the riſk
of the precipice; or much like being left
in the lurch if you declined it, yet, if he
had been a good coachman, I do not ſee
how you could juſtify refuſing him a character. Nay, perhaps, if he had ſerved
you well, and was a favourite in the family,
you would very probably give him and his
wife *ſome little matter* to ſet up with in buſineſs, if they choſe it, on quitting your
place.—This is directly the caſe of our
GREAT MAN—This is the very CAUSE
AND MANNER *of his reſigning the Seals*—
and yet this has been *groſsly miſrepreſented*

in

in the City, as well as the most gracious and spontaneous marks of his Majesty's approbation of his services, which marks, followed *his resignation, infamously traduced as. a Bargain for his forsaking the Publick.* However, heaven be praifed, he is and ever was *little folicitous about the cenfures of the Capricious and the Ungenerous,* and now he is retired from the Administration of public affairs, he is at leisure to pursue his private occupations. He may amuse himself with improving his little income in the alley, with buying out and selling in, and watching the various revolutions of the stocks: or he may lay it out in fashionable improvements of his houfe and gardens at *H—y—s:* or, if amidst the wonderful versatility of his Genius, he has any turn for Trade, he may, if he pleafes, convert his

F   *An-*

Annuity into one large capital, and then, being free of the *Grocer's company*, you know he may go into partnerſhip with his friend the preſent L——d M--y--r, who is the moſt eminent in that buſineſs. In ſuch a caſe, at how many thouſand pounds might the very *good will* of the ſhop be rated at ! Would not all ranks and degrees of people be his cuſtomers ! Would not every Alderman's Cuſtard contain his Sugar and Nutmeg ! Would not the *Sunday's* plum-pudding of every patriot mechanick be filled with his dried currants and raiſins? and would not every publick-ſpirited waſherwoman in town purchaſe her halfquartern of *Bohea* at that ſhop ?

Having travelled thus far in vindication of the Right Honourable ANNUITANT, it

gives

gives me unfpeakable pleafure to find my fentiments of his Letter fall in fo exactly with thofe of the Gentleman in the City, to whom it was addreffed. : The anfwer, which he returned, confiders the matter exactly in the fame light that I have done, the defence that he makes is exactly of the fame colour, and the reafons which he has urged in favour of his friend are equally ftrong and fatisfactory. But take it, as you have had the other, at full length.

LETTER TO A RIGHT HONOUR- ABLE PERSON.

DEAR SIR,

' THE City of *London*, as long as they
' have any Memory, cannot forget,

that

' that you accepted the Seals when the
' Nation was in the moft deplorable Cir-
' cumftances to which any Country can
' be reduced: . That our Armies were
' beaten, our Navy inactive, our Trade
' expofed to the Enemy, our Credit, as if
' we expected to become Bankrupts, funk
' to the loweft Pitch, that there was no-
' thing to be found but Defpondency at
' Home, and Contempt. Abroad. The
' City muft alfo for ever. remember,
' that when you refigned the Seals, our
' Armies and Navies were victorious, our
' Trade fecure, and flourifhing more than
' in a Peace, our Public Credit reftored,
' and People readier to lend than Mini-
' fters to borrow : That there was nothing
' but Exultation at Home, Confufion and
' Defpair among our Enemies, Amaze-
' ment

' ment and Veneration among all Neutral
' Nations: That the *French* were reduced
' so low as to sue for a Peace, which we,
' from Humanity, were willing to grant;
' though their Haughtiness was too great,
' and our Successes too many, for any
' Terms to be agreed on. Remembering
' this, the City cannot but lament that you
' have quitted the Helm. But if Knaves
' have taught Fools to call your Resigna-
' tion, (when you can no longer procure
' the same Success, being prevented from
' pursuing the same Measures) a Desertion
' of the Publick, and to look upon you,
' for accepting a Reward, which can scarce
' bear that Name, in the Light of a Pen-
' sioner; the City of *London* hope, they
' shall not be ranked by you among the
' one or the other. They are truly sensible,

' ble, that, though you ceafe to guide the
' Helm, you have not deferted the Veffel;
' and that, Penfioner as you are, your In-
' clination to promote the publick Good,
' is ftill only to be equalled by your Abi-
' lity : That you fincerely with Succefs to
' the new Pilot, and will be ready, not
' only to warn him and the Crew of Rocks
' and Quickfands, but to affift in bringing
' the Ship through the Storm into a fafe
' Harbour.

" Thefe, Sir, I am perfuaded, are the
" real Sentiments of the City of *London*; I
" am fure you believe them to be fuch of,

DEAR SIR,

Your, &c.

With

With what pathetick energy hath this *anfwering* Citizen recapitulated the great actions of his friend !—The good he has done us by coming into power, the evil that may enfue from his going out, and that he has, it feems, the whole city in a ftring, are circumftances, which, (to ufe the Anfwerer's words) *as long as we have any memory, we cannot forget.* You may perceive alfo in this anfwer fomething of the fame complexion with my illuftration of the Office of Minifter, by the character of a *Coachman*; only that the judicious *Anfwerer* has with the utmoft propriety, in this our maritime nation, tranfported the allufion from land to fea. Obferve his words ! *The* CITY *cannot but lament that you have quitted the* HELM. *But they are truly fenfible, that,*

though

though you ceafe to GUIDE THE HELM, *you have not deferted the veffel :* and that, PENSIONER AS YOU ARE, *your inclina-tion to promote the publick good, is ftill only to be equalled by your Ability : That you fin-cerely wifh fuccefs to the new* PILOT, *and will be ready, not only to warn* HIM *and the* CREW *of* ROCKS *and* QUICKSANDS, *but to affift in bringing the* SHIP *through the* STORM *into a fafe* HARBOUR.—With how much grandeur has the *Anfwerer*, even in the familiarity of the epiftolary ftile, maintained this noble allufion! The allegorical genius of *Bunyan* himfelf could not have purfued it with more ftrict pro-priety and fuccefs; or rather, to raife my comparifon, the *Anfwerer* has rivaled even *Horace* in that exalted Ode, wherein he likens the Commonwealth to a *Ship :*

nay,

nay, he has even furpaffed the *Roman*
Poet, for by adding the *particular Cuftoms*
of our Age and Country to the *general*
turn of the Allufion, which both writers
poffefs in common. with each other, he
has moft wonderfully ftrengthened and
enforced it, and carried it much further
than the *Latin* Lyrick could poffibly do.
It is well known that the noble fpirit of
charity and munificence, fo peculiar to
this country, gave rife to the noble infti-
tutions of *Chelfea* and *Greenwich* Colleges,
for the fupport of decayed Veterans in
our fervice both by land and fea; and it
is alfo further known that the old or difabled foldiers and feamen maintained by
thefe charities are called PENSIONERS.
To this it is that we owe, in the midft of
fuch a cloud of naval terms, the intro-
G   duction.

duction of thofe remarkable words, PEN-
SIONER AS YOU ARE. The elegant Anfwerer, while he confiders the State as a
Ship ; the holding the feals as *guiding the
helm* ; the Minifter as the *Pilot*; the people,
or perhaps only the Members of the H—
of C———ns; as the *Crew* ; bad Meafures
as *Rocks* and *Quickfands* ; War as a *Storm* ;
and Peace - as the *Harbour* ;———at the
fame time heightens the fimilitude by
looking on the Right Honourable. Annuitant as a *Greenwich*-College PENSION-
ER : by which ingenious allufion to our
own imes and manners, he not only
far tranfcends the Simplicity of *Horace*,
but, alfo furnifhes us with an admirable
idea of *Penfioners* in general.. . In both
thefe Colleges, there are what they call
In-PENSIONERS, and *Out*-PENSIONERS—
fome,

some, who conftitute, as it were, the family of the Hofpital, and others who may be faid to be kept on Board-Wages.—And perhaps the only, or at leaft the beft, Reafon, why the whole Band of *Court*-PENSIONERS are not embodied and fupported together in a college of this nature, is, that the number of *In*-PENSIONERS is fo very fmall in comparifon to that of the *Out*-PENSIONERS. The Right Honourable ANNUITANT, having refigned the Seals, is become, like many more of his Cotemporaries and Predeceffors, an *Out*-PENSIONER: but yet, PENSIONER AS HE IS, we are told, that he is not, like the reft of the *College*, a difabled mariner—a decayed veteran that has loft either his ftrength or abilities in the fervice—but one that has both inclination and ability

for

for the public fervice ftill remaining—one
that is ready to *warn*, as well as to *affift*.
——In this new light, wherein the *Anfwerer* has exhibited his friend, he may
be confidered as a broken officer, who is
ftill retained on half-pay, and remains
ready to be called out on any future oc-
cafions of fervice—at leaft he may be faid
to have the benefit of the *College*, while
he is ftill on board the veffel; or, what
is ftill more defirable, he is at liberty to
lie by and receive his pay, or help to work
the Ship, juft as he pleafes. He may
fwing at eafe in his hammock, in the
midft of the ftorm, and content himfelf,
like the *Irifhman*, with faying, *that be is
only a Paffenger*; or he may haul a cable,
reef a fail, make his voice and his whiftle
as rough and as loud as the Boatfwain's,

and

and be as bufy aftern or abaft, below or aloft, as any man in the veffel.——In a word—to fet the fimile adrift, and fpeak in plain terms, our GREAT MAN has now moft *prudently* thrown himfelf into a fitu-ation, in which he may, even with more confiftency than heretofore, embrace any meafures, however oppofite or contradic-tory. He is ready, as the Anfwerer tells us, either to *warn or to affift :* that is, he is ready, juft as occafion fhall ferve, either to acquiefce peaceably in the meafures of the Adminiftration, as other PENSIONERS have done; or elfe to exhibit himfelf to the world in the very new and fingular cha-racter of a PENSIONER IN OPPOSITION — a PATRIOT-PENSIONER, or in its proper and peculiar phrafe, a *Right Honourable* ANNUITANT.

To

To you perhaps, my dear Sir, it may appear ftrange and unaccountable, that he fhould be able to reconcile to each other two fuch contradictory characters; and that while he eats the bread of the court, he fhould oppofe the meafures of the Admini-ftration. But this, Sir, is the diftinguifh-ing excellence of his temper and conduct. Your ftubborn patriotifm, like the needle ftedfaft to the pole, points always one way; but the new mode of patriotifm, like the weathercock changing with every wind, knows how to veer and turn, and is ready to adapt itfelf to times and their feafons, things and their circumftances—*In* or *out*— *for* or *againft*—juft as their convenience fuits, or occafion requires.—*Demofthenes*, the great Orator of *Greece*, forfeited the reputation of integrity, which he had al-

ways

ways maintained till that period, by receiving a bribe from *Harpalus*, in confequence
of which he appeared in the affembly,
muffled about the throat, and made figns,
that he was not able to deliver a Syllable.
It appears from hence, that it was not the
receiving the bribe, but the holding his
peace, by which *Demofthenes* injured his
fame. But our great Orator is ready to
convince the world, that no *Reward* fhall
tie his tongue, or bind his hands; and
that it fhall not be imputed to him, as it
was to *Demofthenes*, that he is affected
with a *Gold* or *Silver Quinfy*.—I have juft
mentioned *Demofthenes*, becaufe in the lift
of patriots it is always ufual to thunder out
a long mufter-roll of *Greek* and *Roman*
Names: but I will venture to fay that there
is no Patriot of all antiquity more eminent

and

and illuftrious, than our Great Commoner has proved himfelf to be in his late Refignation.—If the elder *Brutus* is fo much to be commended, becaufe he could prevail on himfelf to give up the neareft and deareft part of his family to publick juftice, how much more applaufe is due to our modern *Brutus*, who could manifeft his confidence in the publick and love to his family at one and the fame time, by throwing *them*, as well as himfelf, on his country for fupport? If the other old *Roman*, who, when he left the affairs of the publick, retired to his farm and turnips—-But it is vain and needlefs to recur to *Greece* and *Rome* for comparifons, or to draw parallels between the Great Men of Antiquity and thofe of our own times, when we can fo much more properly compare our cotemporary ftatefmen

to

to each other. Indeed, when I confider with how much *prudence* the Right Hon. Annuitant has withdrawn himfelf from bufinefs, juft when it was likely to become moft troublefome;- what a fnug provifion he has acquired for himfelf in his retirement; and how calm and unconcerned he may fit amidft the general hurry and confufion;—I cannot compare him fo juftly to any other object, as to the *other* Great Man, who has fo long been the moft principal director of our affairs. That accomplifhed *M——r,* on a late publick occafion, found himfelf in a fituation exactly parallel to that of our Great Commoner at prefent. In the midft of the noife and buftle of the Coronation, he retired, unobferved by all, to the *Privy Chamber,* where fome ladies of the Court accidentally dif-

H   covered

covered him *eafing himfelf* moft philofo-
phically of every troublefome appendage
to luxury and greatnefs, enjoying the com-
fort of his retreat, *ftraining* beyond the
reach of vulgar faculties, and furrounded
with every fymptom of felicity and *good luck*.

Having accidentally mentioned the *other*
Great Man, I cannot conclude this tedious
Letter, without adding a word or two in
his favour : and as it is the opinion of many
perfons, and, I fear, the invidious wifh
of many more, that he likewife will fhortly
find it expedient to *refign*, I think that the
Crown and the People are each bound in
honour and gratitude to make *him*, alfo a
handfome appointment, as well as the Right
Hon. Annuitant. It would be hard indeed,
as *Mat Prior* has it, *if one moufe eats while*

t'other

t'other starves; or that we fhould take fuch
provident care of our *right-hand* Statefman,
and leave our helplefs *left-handed* Minifter
in the lurch; fince he is at leaft a *limb* of
the *body politick*, though not of equal ufe
with his *fellow*. He has been fo grofsly
reviled for the wretched peace, which he
hammered out for us in 1748; that I doubt
he will fcarce try his hand to *tinker up* another. I beg leave therefore (as I own myfelf under obligations to him) to urge a few
arguments in his behalf, to fhew why he
ought to be allowed at leaft as good a *Pen-*
fion, if an *Annuity* be thought too peculiar
an indulgence, as any of thofe eminent per-
fonages, who have lately been removed:
and I much queftion, notwithftanding the
great number of his own extraordinary
largeffes of this nature, whether he will

find

find many men, befides myfelf, thus grate-
ful to him, when he is out of Power. And
the firft general Reafon I will prefume to
-give, is this :

That it would be a difgrace indeed upon the Government and the whole nation,
if *he alone* fhould go unrewarded for his
long, wonderful, and inexpreffible fervices. I believe I may venture to affert,
that fcarce any body of late has been difmif-
fed without *this publick mark of approbation
following their refignation.*--And why fhould
he ?——Some, perhaps, who belong to
the honourable lift of Penfioners, have had
their names more carefully and *prudently*
concealed than others ; but if the truth
was known, and a fair and honeft Regifter
of *Penfioners* was made out, and laid before
the

the Publick, I am perfuaded, we fhould
find many great and worthy names, that
have long lain dormant, and fuch as few,
except the honourable fraternity themfelves,
ever could fufpect.

Another ftrong argument in his favour
is, that he has been as long in a *lucrative
employment*, if not longer, than moft of his
predeceffors or cotemporaries, and confe-
quently deferves as large, if not a larger
Penfion, than any of them.—This is but
ftrict juftice according to the invariable
golden rule of modern politicks.

A further reafon for putting this act of gratitude fpeedily in execution, is, that, fuch of
late has been the profufion of grants of this
nature, that there is fome doubt whether

there

there will otherwife be treafure fufficient to anfwer fo large a demand left in the Exch—r. It may be neceffary perhaps, on this occafion, to call in aid *another kingdom*, which is tolerably well loaded already, and will fcarce be able to receive many more of thefe worthy gentlemen, fent over by this *honorary* kind of *tranfportation*. And, by the bye, I cannot help thinking, that our Great Men ingrafted on that ftock, ought to carry fome diftinguifhing mark of their belonging to that country. Suppofe, therefore, that, in thefe cafes, a Silver Badge of S. P. for *St. Patrick*, fhould be worn on the left fhoulder; and when any perfons are provided for on the *home lift*, I would have a golden badge for the Right fhoulder, with S. G. upon it, for *St. George*, with the additional honour to the Wearers,

that

their names and *titles*, written in capitals, should be hung up in *St. George*'s chapel above the lift of the Poor Knights of *Windfor*.—But to return ;

Whilft I have been inadvertently tempted to expatiate on the general nature of thefe largeffes, this very digreffion has fuggefted to me the ftrongeft argument in behalf of this Great M——r.—— To fum up every reafon that can be urged in one fhort queftion, let me only afk you, whether it would not be a moft unnatural reproach on the gratitude of the nation, if that perfon, who has generoufly beftowed fo many great and honourable *Penfions*, fhould remain in want of one himfelf? *Petimufque damufque viciffim*, fays that honeft verfe of *Horace*, founded in gratitude. This, I think, fhould be the Motto of the whole *Band*, and fhould be ftuck up in a confpicuous part of the Beef-eater's room at court, to fhew every body, as they enter, what favours Statefmen may expect from each other : and the fame device might be properly ufed in another *certain place* for the information of young m——rs.—Upon the principles of this axiom, the expedient I would propofe to provide for this Great Man, is, that every L——d or C——r in this Kingdom, or the neighbouring one, poffeft of a Penfion, exceeding 1000 *l. per* year, fhould, by way of poundage, make him an allowance of 5 *l. per cent.*—and then *be* too will perhaps be provided for, pretty near equal to his merits—more at leaft than any other perfon—as well as have both his fhoulders properly decorated, according to the abovementioned Propofal.

Ha-

Having thus endeavoured (as bound in gratitude) to carve out a handſome proviſion for this Great Man, as well as the other, it is high time to conclude. I cannot however take my final leave of you, without lamenting the general deſpondency which you tell me the *Seceſſion* of the Right Honourable Annuitant occaſions in the Country. Much of it appears alſo in town : but in my mind it argues a poor and mean ſpirit, unworthy of *Britons,* unworthy of men. Have we, for Heaven's Sake, but ONE honeſt and able man among us? I ſhould be ſorry to hear even our enemies ſay ſo. I will venture to ſay that there is at leaſt ONE MORE, of whom I have a better opinion, than even of our Great Man. The Perſon I mean is no other than THE KING. He has al-

                I   ready

ready manifested the truest affection for his people : and why should we be alarmed or disturbed at the cabals and intrigues of our *fellow-servants*, when we are assured of the care and protection of our MASTER? He knows the just limits by which his Power is circumscribed, and desires not to enlarge its bounds. In like manner let every officer of state honestly perform the duties of his place, and aim at nothing more! While they bawl in opposition, they complain that power is dangerous in the hands of a Minister; but when they get into power themselves, they dare to complain of being manacled and fettered. The Power of the *British* Constitution is lodged in no ONE Man, or Set of Men, but collectively in the Whole People. It were to be wished, therefore, by all

HONEST MEN, that this frightful *Chimæra*
of a PRIME MINISTER—GREAT MAN—
or whatever he may call himfelf—that has
fo long ftalked between the Throne and
the people in this nation, were totally
annihilated: and as is generally faid, that,
at the late Coronation, his prefent Majefty found himfelf obliged to be *his own*
BISHOP, *his own* HERALD, *&c.* happy
would it be for *Great Britain,* if it fhould
prove an Omen that in this aufpicious
reign, He will be found alfo to prove
HIS OWN MINISTER.

I am, my Dear Sir,

Your, &c.

POST-

POSTSCRIPT.

October 22, 1761.

I Cannot forbear the triumph of adding
a Postscript to transmit immediately to
you the following Paragraph from the *St.
James's* Chronicle of this Evening.

*At a Court of Common Council held this
Day at Guildhall, a Motion was made, that
an Address should be presented to the Right
Hon. William Pitt, Esq; for his past Ser-
vices. After several Speeches against the
Motion, by a learned Deputy, the Ques-*

tion

tion was put; and upon holding up of Hands, there appeared

For addreſſing Mr. Pitt - - 109

Againſt it - - - - - - - - 15

Whereupon a Committee was appointed to draw up the ſaid Addreſs; and alſo, at the ſame Time, to requeſt of Mr. Pitt, that he would continue to purſue the ſame Patriotick Principles upon which he has hitherto acted.

This, I hope, will thoroughly convince you Country-gentlemen of your error. Our honeſt Citizens, you ſee, know his merits : and though his name, as an *Annuitant*, has been publiſhed and printed, like the Bankrupts, in the *London Gazette*, yet the ſagacious Common

mon Council have no lefs opinion of his being a *good Man* on that account. Perhaps they confider a Statefman, who becomes a PENSIONER as a *broken Patriot*—a *Bankrupt* in Politicks—and it is not to be doubted but the Right Honourable ANNUITANT will convince them, that fuch a man, like *other* Bankrupts, can fet up again, and drive a more thriving trade than ever he did before.

F I N I S.